Fun with Dick and Jane

A COMMEMORATIVE COLLECTION OF STORIES

ScottForesman
A Division of HarperCollins*Publishers*

The first Dick and Jane story appeared in Scott Foresman's 1930 Elson Basic Readers Pre-Primer. For the next forty years, these simple stories taught millions of children to read with their basic vocabulary, warmly drawn pictures and endearing plots. Many things have changed since then, but Scott Foresman remains committed to America's teachers and students. To celebrate our centennial, we're happy to present you with this sampling of classic Dick and Jane stories.

Look

Look, look.

Oh, oh, oh.

Oh, oh.

Oh, look.

Spot

Come, Dick.

Come and see.

Come, come.

Come and see.

Come and see Spot.

Look, Spot.

Oh, look.

Look and see.

Oh, see.

Run, Spot.

Run, run, run.

Oh, oh, oh.

Funny, funny Spot.

See It Go

Jane said, "Look, look.

I see a big yellow car.

See the yellow car go."

Sally said, "I see it.

I see the big yellow car.

I want to go away in it.

I want to go away, away."

Dick said, "Look up, Sally.

You can see something.

It is red and yellow.

It can go up, up, up.

It can go away."

Sally said, "I want to go up.

I want to go up in it.

I want to go up, up, up.

I want to go up and away."

"Look, Sally," said Dick.

"Here is Father in a boat.

You can go away in it."

"Jump in, jump in," said Father.

"Jump in the big blue boat."

"We can go," said Sally.

"We can go away in a boat.

Away in a big blue boat."

A Doll for Jane

"Hello, Father," said Dick.

"Jane will have a birthday soon.

Please get a new doll for Jane.

Get a baby doll that talks.

Please get a doll that talks."

Sally said, "Oh, Mother.

Jane will have a birthday.

She will have a birthday soon.

Guess what Jane wants.

She wants a new doll.

She saw a baby doll that talks.

She wants it.

Please get a baby doll for Jane."

"Happy birthday," said Father.

"I have something for you, Jane."

"Happy birthday!" said Mother.

"Happy birthday, Jane.

I have something for you, too."

Jane said, "Thank you, Father.

Thank you, Mother.

I cannot guess what you

have for my birthday."

"Here, Jane," said Dick.

"This is something for you."

Jane ran to Dick.

"Oh, is that for me?" she said.

"Is that for my birthday, too?

I cannot guess what it is.

I will look and see."

"One, two, three," said Jane.

"Three new dolls for my birthday!

Three baby dolls that talk!

All for my birthday!

Now I have a big doll family.

Thank you, thank you, thank you.

This is a happy birthday.

A happy, happy birthday for me."

Something Blue for Puff

"Girls! Girls!" said Dick.

"Come in the house.

I want you to see something."

Pam said, "Oh, Dick!

What do you want us to see?"

"Come and find out," said Dick.

"It is something you girls will like."

Dick said, "See what Mike and I have.

This is Puff with me.

That is Spot with Mike."

Mike said, "Come here, girls.

See Spot and Puff in a little play."

"Oh, I like plays," said Sally.

"We do, too," said Pam and Penny.

Spot said, "Hello, Puff.

See my red coat.

Do you want a red coat, too?"

Puff said, "I like the red coat, Spot.

But I want a blue coat.

Maybe you can find a blue one for me."

"That is easy," said Spot.

"Look at my hat and you will see."

"Puff! Look at this!" said Spot.

"Here is a blue coat for you!"

Penny said, "Oh, that is good, Spot!

Now find coats for us!

Find a blue coat for Sally.

Find red coats for Pam and me."

The stories in this commemorative collection come from the following New Basic Readers books: p. 3 "Look," *The New We Look and See*, 1951; p.7 "Spot," *Look and See*, 1946; p. 11 "See It Go," *The New We Come and Go*, 1951; p. 15 "A Doll for Jane," *The New Fun with Dick and Jane*, 1951, p. 20 "Something Blue for Puff," *Fun with Our Friends*, 1965.

Copyright ©1996 Scott, Foresman and Company

The New We Look and See and *The New We Come and Go* by William S. Gray, A. Sterl Artley and May Hill Arbuthnot. Illustrated by Eleanor Campbell. Copyright 1951, renewed 1979 by Scott, Foresman and Company.

The New Fun with Dick and Jane by William S. Gray, A. Sterl Artley and May Hill Arbuthnot. Illustrated by Keith Ward and Eleanor Campbell. Copyright 1951, renewed 1979 by Scott, Foresman and Company.

Fun with Our Friends by Helen M. Robinson, Marion Monroe, A. Sterl Artley, Charlotte S. Huck and William A. Jenkins. Illustrated by Bob Childress and Jack White. Copyright ©1965 by Scott, Foresman and Company.

ISBN: 0–673–32271–8
Printed in China